JAKE IN SPACE

To my dad, for inspiring
my own sense of adventure.

First published in the UK in 2017
by New Frontier Publishing (Europe) Pty. Ltd.
93 Harbord Street, London SW6 6PN
www.newfrontierpublishing.co.uk

ISBN: 978-1-912076-00-0

A CIP catalogue record for this book is available from the British Library.

Printed in China
10 9 8 7 6 5 4 3 2 1

Cover illustration and design by Celeste Hulme

JAKE
IN SPACE
MOON ATTACK

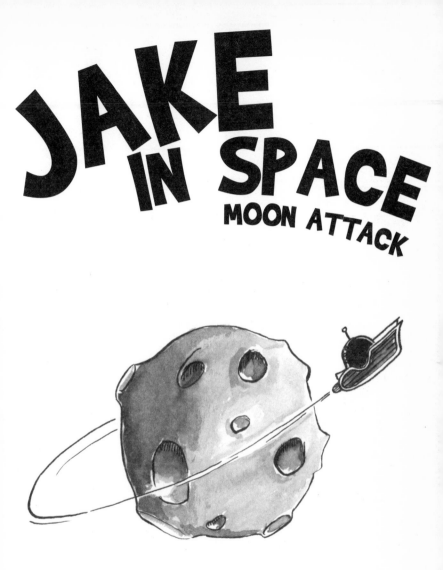

Candice Lemon-Scott
Illustrated by Celeste Hulme

Welcome, Jake.

I am pleased to let you know that you have been accepted into the Remedial Space Car Driving School program for failed drivers.

I am so sure that you will pass your driving test by the end of the week that if you don't, you will get your money back.

Please be at the Remedial Space Car Driving School, located at Moon Base entrance 303, at 2pm sharp on Friday 13 October 4040.

Please bring:
* zero-gravity wear
* infra-red goggles
* suction bowl.

The following items are <u>not allowed</u>:
* real reality computer games
* disguising gel
* lollies — including all exploding and vanishing types.

I look forward to meeting you.
Space thoughts and wishes,

Gradock

Gradock.

emedial Space Car Driving School! *Remedial!* Jake thought. *Why didn't Mum and Dad just put a big sticker on my forehead that said 'Universe's Biggest Loser?'* He scrunched the letter up in an angry fist and threw it back at his parents – except the letter stuck fast to his fingers. He tried to shake it off but the paper just seemed to hold on tighter to his skin.

'It's Slooper Goo. We thought you might

1

react this way,' Mum said, shrugging.

'There's no getting out of it,' Dad added. 'You *have* to get that licence.'

'But *remedial* school? How could you do this to me? Everyone at school will find out,' Jake said, still trying to remove the letter from his fingers.

'You've failed your licence thirty times. Sorry, but we're not going to drive you around for the rest of your life,' Mum replied.

'I'll get it next time. I promise.' Jake put his hand in the kitchen sink. 'Water.'

Jets of cold water sprayed from tiny holes in the sink. He waited for the water to soak his hand before pulling it out again, but the letter just became a sticky lump in his fist. His fingers started to ache.

'You're eleven now. How many kids get driven to school at that age?' Dad said.

Jake had to admit that it *was* pretty

2

embarrassing getting dropped off at school by his parents. Even his best friends were driving, and they were nearly six months younger than him. And then there was his space car, sitting in mid-air, never being used except for driving lessons.

'Maybe I just need a new driving instructor?' Jake said, hopefully.

'You know we've already tried every instructor on Earth,' Mum answered.

Jake knew remedial school was his only chance to get his licence. But he knew it would be boring spending a whole week on the Moon. There was nothing there except for a heap of rocks and craters.

'Gradock is the best. No-one has ever failed his driving school,' Dad added.

Jake knew he was right but he still didn't know what was worse: being driven to school or having his whole class know he had to go to remedial. Sometimes he wished he lived in the atmosphere like heaps of other kids did. Instead, he was stuck on a space station.

'We're not giving you a choice, Jake,' Mum said.

Jake hated it when his mum used telepathy on him. Just because in the history books mums had special instincts, he didn't think they should be allowed to know *everything* about their kids. Mum said she only used telepathy in emergencies, but there seemed to be a lot of emergencies lately.

'We need to leave in half an hour. You'd better get packing.'

'But ...'

'You're going and that's final,' Dad stated.

Jake knew there was no getting out of it. Sadly, he held up the fist that still had the letter stuck fast to it with the Slooper Goo.

'Oh, right,' Mum said. She handed Jake a jar

full of neon red gas. 'Put your hand in that.'

Frowning, he stuck his fist in the jar. He felt the paper melting. He pulled his hand back out, cracking his knuckles as he stretched his fingers again, then crossed the kitchen to the room teleportation chair.

He put his hands on the sensors. 'Bedroom,' he snapped at the cartoon face on the computer screen in front of him.

He hit the eject button and teleported to his room.

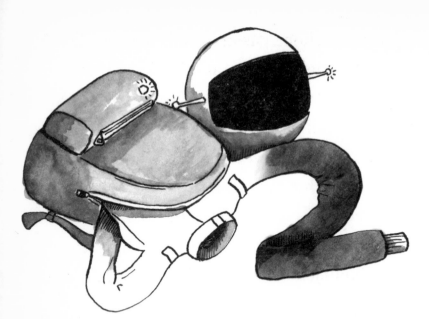

Before long Jake was in orbit and headed straight for the Moon. It was a few minutes before two o'clock when the Remedial Space Car Driving School entrance came into view.

The Moon looked just the same as it did in Jake's schoolbooks: grey, rocky and dusty. He knew it was going to be a long week, especially without so much as a real reality computer game to play with. The driving school

6

building shone silver. Jake's dad explained that the metal foil was used to keep the inside temperature even. Jake nodded, distracted, as his family's dusty red space car screeched to a stop above a bright blue, brand-new Space 4041 with hydropower.

'Careful – you nearly hit that car,' Mum warned Dad.

'I had plenty of room. Look at all that space below.'

'Well, at least we know where Jake *didn't* get his driving skills from,' Mum said, seeming to forget Jake was sitting in the back seat.

'At least I don't forget where I put my remote key entry lock all the time,' Dad snapped.

'At least I didn't fail my driving test fifty-four times,' Mum snapped back.

Suddenly Jake's parents remembered he was there and they both turned and grinned at him.

'We were just joking around, weren't we?' Dad quickly said to Mum.

Jake's mum grinned and nodded. He was starting to think that having a week at remedial school wouldn't be so bad after all. At least now he'd have something to say if his dad made any more comments about the number of times he had failed his test.

Dad hit the exit button and the car doors flew open. Jake and his parents stepped onto the platform leading to the main entrance of the building, then bounced along towards the huge metal doors. Mum was fascinated by the swirls of dust that blew up on the surface of the Moon. *Great, Mum – maybe you'd prefer to spend the week here instead*, thought Jake grumpily.

He looked behind him. The family from the 4041 space car was following them towards the school doors. The boy had jet-black hair that was so straight and short it looked like it had been ironed flat against his head. Jake thought his mum would be happy if his hair did that instead of frizzing out in a brown ball whenever he hit zero gravity. Jake noticed the boy was dressed all in black too and his body was covered in a filmy-looking material. Jake realised he must be wearing the new 'all temperatures' space suit that had just come out. The boy's mum and dad were dressed in the new space suits too. His mum was wearing an emerald green one, and his dad a ruby red one.

'Is this where I'm to stay during the remedial program?' the boy said.

'Yes, Henry, this is the Remedial Space Car Driving School,' his mum replied.

'Very well. What is the time frame?'

'One week,' Henry's dad said. 'Only one week and you'll be well rewarded. Well rewarded, son.'

Jake thought they talked pretty weirdly but he guessed not all families were like his. The boy called Henry bounced straight past him and entered the building. He didn't even say goodbye to his parents as the doors opened and closed in front of them.

'I suppose this is as far as we go, then,' Mum said once they'd reached the main entrance airlock. She smoothed down Jake's bulky space suit. 'I'm sure the week will be gone before you can say "moon dust".'

'Sure, Mum.'

'Take it easy and listen to Gradock,' Dad said.

Jake stepped forward. The entry doors slid upwards and he walked through. He turned to wave to his mum and dad just as the doors slid shut once more. *Sloop!* The airlocks closed and then his parents were gone. He suddenly felt very alone.

There were about fifteen other kids already in the foyer. Some seemed to know each other, while others had formed quiet groups. Jake took off his space suit and stuffed it into his backpack. It felt good to be able to move freely and breathe easily again. He noticed another boy standing by a corner with his backpack at his feet. Jake went over to him, glad not to be the only one on his own.

'Hi, I'm Jake from Earth,' he said.

'Can you believe this place?' the boy replied. 'It's so, so … *clean*. I bet they use those roving robot mops over the whole place. The walls are so shiny! I'm Rory from Mars, by the way.'

Before they had a chance to say any more a booming voice echoed through the foyer: 'Welcome, recruits.'

The whole room became one giant digital imaging screen. Gradock's huge, mushroom-shaped head covered every wall. He smiled, showing two rows of crystal teeth. Jake noticed that he had a long scar running from the corner of his mouth to his cheekbone, making him look like he was sneering.

'We will begin with your first space car driving lesson. Please pass through the identification screens now,' he boomed.

Gradock's face vanished. They were once more surrounded by the blank, shiny walls.

'What does he mean, "identification screens"?' Jake asked Rory.

Rory shrugged. Then there was another big booming sound and the far wall disappeared, creating an entrance into the main building. A gigantic clear screen came up from the floor, dividing the entrance in half.

'I guess that's it,' Rory said.

The two boys grabbed their bags and headed towards the screen. Jake was glad he had found someone to hang out with.

12

As everyone passed through the left side of the screen Jake heard the echoing sound of a voice calling out names: 'Skye ... Milly ... Henry ...' Every now and then a banned item, like a pack of lollies or a tube of disguising gel, flew through the air and then disappeared. Jake was glad he had decided not to try to sneak in his real reality space monster game. He would hate to lose that.

The next room was even bigger than the foyer and everyone spread out. Jake saw that Rory's mouth was so wide open it looked like he was about to swallow the whole universe. Against one wall there were six big black machines. Everyone started talking noisily about them.

'What are they?' Rory asked.

'I don't know,' Jake replied. 'Maybe they're a new kind of robot.'

As if answering their question, Gradock's

13

booming voice rang out again. 'By the back wall you will find the space car simulators. Please break up into groups of three and select one each.'

'Simulators?' Rory cried, disappointed.

Jake could hear the other students groaning as they formed their groups. Everyone seemed to feel the same.

'How are we meant to learn to drive properly if we don't even get to drive a *real* car?' Jake complained.

'This is going to be more boring than when my class learned about space bug habitats,' Rory agreed.

They were so busy complaining that they didn't notice that someone else had come to join their group.

'I'm Henry from, um, from Jupiter. I will become part of this group because you are two and I am one, and together we make three.'

'I guess so,' Rory said, frowning.

'I'm Jake. This is Rory,' Jake answered.

'Very nice to meet with you,' Henry said.

'Right,' Jake replied. He could tell it was going to be a very long week.

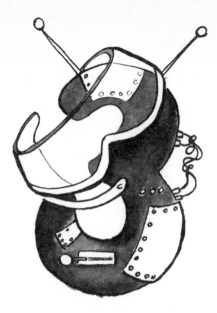

Rory, Henry and Jake slid into the three seats in front of the big, blank screen of the simulator. Then the door closed and everything went black. They all put on their infra-red goggles. Then a screen lit up. They were now looking at a fake surface of the Moon. Jake felt his seat begin to shudder. A voice came over the speaker. Rory jumped.

'We are about to take off into orbit. Please fasten your seatbelts now.'

'Wow, I thought that was my mum for a minute,' Rory laughed.

'Yeah, it sounds so real, hey?' Jake replied.

'That is exactly the purpose of simulators,' Henry explained. 'They copy real life. Have you not experienced this before?'

'Of course not,' Rory and Jake said together.

'Ah, yes. What I meant was, everyone knows what simulators are, do they not?' he said, scrunching his face up like a clump of freeze-dried cereal.

Rory rolled his eyes. Then Jake started floating up from his seat.

'Quick, put your seatbelt on,' Rory said.

He grabbed Jake's arm to hold him down while Jake belted himself in. He felt his hair starting to rise from the top of his head.

'Check out your hair, Jake. You look like you just got zapped.'

Jake looked over at Rory. His blonde hair

was shooting out at all kinds of weird angles. 'Speak for yourself!'

Rory felt the top of his head.

'You require some no-gravity hair wax,' Henry said.

Jake looked at Henry. His hair was still flat on his head. There wasn't a strand of it sticking up anywhere.

'Where do you get no-gravity hair wax from?' Jake asked.

But before Henry could answer the loudspeaker came back on. 'Reaching zero gravity in approximately two seconds.'

The screen changed and they were in darkness again. The only light in the simulator came from the stars shining on the screen. Then the machine started rocking from side to side.

'What are we supposed to do now?' Rory asked.

'Drive this spacecraft, of course,' Henry replied.

'How?' Jake asked.

The rocking became faster and Jake found it hard to stay upright in his seat.

'There is a set of dials and levers in front of our seats. This copies a space car dashboard,' Henry said.

As though hearing him, the loudspeaker voice came on again. 'You will notice a set of dials in front of your seats. These can be used in the same way as the controls in a real space car.'

'I can't see any,' Rory said.

At that moment part of the screen disappeared and a control panel flipped down in front of them.

'How did you know about these?' Jake asked Henry.

'Let's call it a lucky dip,' Henry said.

'A *what*?' Jake said.

'I think he means a lucky guess,' Rory explained.

Then they were pushed sideways. The control panel in front of Henry lit up. It was his turn to drive first. He reached out and pushed a lever. Soon they were flying straight again.

'Good move,' Jake said.

'Thank you,' Henry grinned.

As Henry drove the simulator, Jake started to wonder why Henry was even at remedial school. He seemed too good at driving to need it. He could tell Rory was thinking the same thing. Especially since he frowned every time Henry smoothly veered around a fake space particle.

When Henry swerved around an incoming asteroid and the simulator hardly even tilted, Jake decided to ask him. 'Henry, why are you

at remedial? Your driving is better than my dad's. Not that it's saying a lot, but still you seem too good to have failed your licence.'

Henry was so busy taking them through a pretend dust storm that Jake wondered if he'd even heard him at first. Then his eyes started darting about as though he was trying to read the answer from inside his brain. 'I, um, I suffer from extreme levels of, um, nervousness when driving.'

'Oh, okay. Sorry, I didn't mean to stick my nose in.'

'Where did you stick your nose?' Henry asked.

'Never mind. I was just curious.'

Jake's control panel lit up and he took over from Henry. He steered around a few fake asteroids, barely missing the third one. The course became even harder and he had to steer through clouds of moon dust. Jake hit an asteroid and the simulator vibrated.

It was Rory's turn next. Jake thought he was pretty good at avoiding obstacles but he kept getting a warning light for driving too high.

Before long the screen blacked out and the lights in the simulator came back on. Jake's hair flattened back on his head in a tangled mess. He felt heavy in his chair as gravity returned.

The loudspeaker came back on. 'Thank you everyone. Please unfasten your seatbelts and exit the simulator. You may make your way to the lunchroom, through the red doors to your left.'

Jake climbed out of the simulator. He was pretty pleased with their score, even though it was mostly thanks to Henry. Still, something about Henry felt odd to Jake. Was it just the way he talked, like he was reading from a book? Maybe ... but Jake still thought there was something more. Jake followed Rory, who looked like he couldn't get away from Henry fast enough.

Jake was so tired after his first day of remedial school that he didn't even know he'd fallen asleep until he was woken by a thump in the middle of the night. At first he thought he was home in his bed. Then he remembered where he was: in the boys' dormitory at the Remedial Space Car Driving School. On the Moon.

It was pitch black. Jake unzipped his sleeping bag, felt around for his backpack and pulled out his infra-red goggles. He could see a pair of boots heading towards the door. A hand reached up and covered the identification scan screen, then the door slid open.

Jake couldn't imagine who would be getting up in the middle of the night or why. There wasn't exactly much happening at remedial school after dark. He leaped down from his bed and followed.

Outside the dormitory he looked up and down the long white corridor. At first he couldn't see anyone. Then he spotted a dark shape moving around the corner. He raced after whoever it was. The person had stopped in front of one of the many doors running off the corridor. The door slid open. Jake quickly caught up and made it through just as the door was closing.

Even through his goggles, it was hard for Jake to make things out in the darkness. Not that

25

there seemed to be much to look at anyway. He found himself in a huge, empty room. Whoever he was following stopped once he reached the opposite end of the room. Jake felt his way along the back wall. At first he couldn't see anything but as he got a little closer, he could make out the shape of an airlock. Jake watched the person move towards it and put his hand on the identification screen. The slicked-back hair and stiff walk gave away who it was. It was Henry.

The airlock opened and Henry disappeared through it. Jake followed after him quietly but just as he reached the door it closed tight. Jake pushed on the door. It was locked. He put his hand on the identification screen but nothing happened. He couldn't get through.

Jake peered through the small window at the top of the door. As Henry looked over his right shoulder Jake quickly ducked down out of sight.

26

Jake moved to the side of the room. There was a round window and he peeked out of it. At first all he could see was the grey surface of the Moon and little puffs of dust blowing up. He realised Henry must still be inside the airlock chamber. Then he heard the *sloop* of another airlock opening … and then he could see Henry. He was out on the Moon, in the middle of the night. But why? And how did he know about the hidden exit?

Jake looked closer and couldn't believe what he saw.

Henry wasn't wearing a space suit.

But that wasn't possible. He didn't have any oxygen! Then Henry turned around suddenly. Worried he'd been spotted, Jake stepped backwards and ran back to the dormitory the way he had come.

A million thoughts zoomed through Jake's head like asteroids as he tiptoed as fast as he could down the long corridor. He couldn't understand why Henry had sneaked off in the middle of the night. What had he been doing out on the Moon? Had he seen Jake looking through the window?

Jake put his hand over the dormitory sensor. But just as he was waiting for the door to open he felt a hand clamp firmly on his shoulder. He spun around, sure that Henry had caught him spying and wondering what he could say to him.

But it wasn't Henry – it was the night guard.

'What are you doing out here?' the guard barked.

Jake thought about telling him about Henry. But then he'd have to explain what he was doing following him in the first place. He decided not to say anything.

'Well?' the night guard demanded.

'Ah … I was busting. Have to go. Sorry.'

'Do you want to eat with us?' Rory asked.

'Sure,' Milly said.

Twenty minutes later they were standing in front of four super racer space cars. Jake was so nervous he could feel his breakfast trying to make its way back out of his stomach. This time they had to make groups of five. Rory, Milly, Skye and Henry all joined in with Jake.

'Maybe the simulator wasn't so bad after all,' Jake said to Rory.

'Yeah, at least if we crashed *that* it didn't wreck anything.'

'It is simple to operate once you understand the functions correctly,' Henry interrupted.

Jake could see Milly and Skye trying to hold back a giggle at the way Henry talked, only they weren't doing too well.

'Was it something I said?' Henry asked.

'Or some way you said it,' Rory said, clapping Henry on the back.

Henry moved away from Rory's touch.

'Wow, you must work out a lot,' Rory said. 'Your back feels like metal!'

'Yes, um, exercise is most important for good muscle building.'

Skye whispered in Jake's ear, 'Is he serious?'

'Yeah, I think he is,' Jake whispered back.

They all climbed into the space car.

'You're first,' Rory told Henry.

Jake thought the day was starting out pretty well. He didn't have to drive first, and it didn't look like Henry knew he'd been followed last night.

On their first team flight, Henry did a full orbit of the Moon without hitting any asteroids or going off-course once. He didn't seem to notice anyone else. They were all so relaxed it was like being taken on a joy flight. Milly even took out a pack of space jubes.

'Catch them if you can,' she said, opening

the packet and throwing them into the air.

The lollies floated around the space car and they all chased them, trying to catch them in their hands. Rory even caught one with his foot. One flew in front of Henry. He hit it away and it floated towards Skye, who caught it in her mouth.

'I suspect you shall find that lolly eating while moving is a banned activity.'

'Lighten up,' Rory said, annoyed. 'It's just a bit of fun. And anyway, at least *we're* here because we need to be.'

Everyone went quiet. The rest of the lollies floated around, uneaten.

'I don't understand the meaning of that comment,' Henry replied, swerving around a star.

'You drive perfectly. Why are you at remedial? When we were in the simulator you said it was because you get nervous when you drive for real. Is that true?' Rory asked.

If Henry's pale skin could have turned any paler it would have. His eyes started shifting all around like they had in the simulator. Suddenly his hands began to shake, and he got a weird twitch in the corner of his mouth. Before anyone could say anything Henry lost control of the car and they started heading straight towards the Moon's surface.

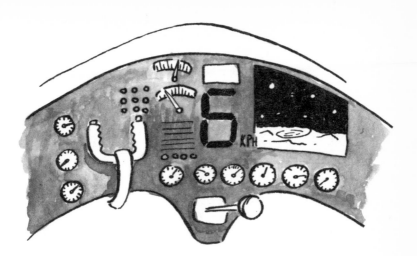

Jake started to wish Rory had kept his mouth shut as the space car headed straight down. Henry must have forgotten all about being scared of driving until Rory reminded him. The Moon came up faster and faster, and if they hadn't all been buckled in they'd have been squashed against the front window. The space car was heading straight towards the grey, rocky surface of the Moon.

'Come in slower,' Rory commanded.

'I can't move my leg,' Henry cried.

They kept gaining speed. The space car started to wobble.

'You're going too fast!' Jake exclaimed.

'We're going to crash!' Skye yelled.

Milly started screaming.

But Henry still didn't move. A huge crater came closer. They were heading straight for it. Jake took over from Henry and pushed the lever over to the left. The space car levelled out and they just made it over the top of the crater. They were still too low to the ground, though, and were thrown forward as the space car hit a huge moon rock. The car flipped onto its side and skidded along the surface of the Moon. Milly was still screaming.

'We're headed straight for the school!' Rory yelled.

Jake saw the big metal building coming

closer and closer as they skidded along.

'Quick, everyone grab onto something,' Skye said.

Jake held tight onto the back of the chair. He closed his eyes, waiting for impact. Then they came to a stop.

'Emergency braking system is now engaged,' a computerised voice said through the intercom.

'Couldn't it have *engaged* a bit sooner?' Rory said.

Jake opened his eyes and looked out the window. All he could see was a wall of silver. Any closer and they would have crashed straight into the school.

'It seems I do still get nervous driving,' Henry said.

No-one said anything as they all crawled out of one of the windows and headed towards the school. At least they all believed Henry now.

Inside, they were met with the image of Gradock's serious face projected around the foyer. A group of students was staring quietly up at the screens as he spoke.

'... and let that be a lesson to you all about how important space car driving safety is.'

His eyes flickered over to Jake's group. 'Ah, here they are now. I hope you have all learned how important it is to work as a team and to concentrate at all times when driving. Eating lollies while in space is a very easy way to get distracted. That's all. Theory lesson two will be after lunch.'

The screen went blank. Jake felt sick. What a terrible start to his second day. Right now, he'd be lucky to make it through the week at remedial school, let alone pass the driving test at the end of it.

Rory and Jake filled their bowls with vegetable stew and sat at one of the tables. They pushed their mushy meal around their plates with their forks. Neither of them felt like eating after their crash landing, not to mention being told off by Gradock about driving safety.

Jake looked up to see Henry heading towards them. Henry waved but Jake pretended he hadn't seen him. When he reached their table he smiled as though nothing had happened and went to sit next to Rory. But Rory was quick to put his hand down on the chair.

'Sorry, that seat's for someone else.'

Henry shrugged and went to sit next to Jake instead but Rory slapped his hand down again.

'That one too.'

Henry did his face-crunch thing and Jake started to feel a bit sorry for him.

'I shall rack off then, shall I?'

'Good idea,' Rory said.

Henry walked away.

'And no-one says "rack off" anymore,' Rory yelled after him.

Jake turned to Rory. 'He didn't mean it, you know.'

'Yes, he did! He was actually going to sit with us after getting us into trouble. And he nearly killed us, in case you've forgotten.'

'No, I mean he didn't try to kill us.'

'Then how do you explain him going from perfect driving to crash landing in two nanoseconds?'

Jake leaned in close to Rory. 'There's something I've been wanting to tell you about Henry.'

'Besides him being a complete dork?'

'I'm serious,' Jake said in a whisper. He started explaining to Rory how he had followed Henry the night before. 'Then he went through the airlock. I couldn't get in so I looked through the window. He was outside.'

'So?' Rory said.

'He wasn't wearing a space suit.'

Rory stopped pushing his food around. 'Very funny.'

'I'm serious. He just had his indoor clothes on. No space suit. No oxygen mask. Nothing.'

'But that's impossible!'

'Is this a two-person party or can anyone

43

join?' Milly put her tray down next to Rory's. Skye sat down next to Jake. 'You look pale,' Milly said, staring at Rory.

'I still feel a bit sick. At least I know I'm not the worst driver at remedial anymore.'

'What were you two talking about anyway?' asked Skye.

Jake was about to tell Skye about Henry. Her dark brown eyes looked worried, and Jake knew he could trust her. But Rory kicked him under the table.

'You looked like you were talking about something serious,' Skye prodded.

'It was nothing. Just boy talk. You know,' Rory said.

'Boring,' Milly said, laughing.

Skye was still looking at Jake as though she knew there was more to it than that. Jake stared down at his plate, feeling his face burning hotter than the sun.

That night Jake decided to stay awake to see if Henry was going to sneak out of the dorm again. Rory and Jake kept their space suits folded underneath their pillows, ready to follow him if he tried to go out on the Moon. Rory still didn't believe Henry could have been out there without a space suit on. But Jake knew what he had seen.

He lay in bed thinking about Henry and the crash and Gradock telling them they had to work as a team. And the next thing he knew, it was early morning.

It seemed that Henry hadn't snuck out this time – or at least Jake had been fast asleep if he had. He looked over at Rory but Rory just shook his head.

After breakfast a robot led them along a winding corridor to the space car loading zone. Rory, Milly, Skye and Jake were all quiet. Their driving test was only a few days away.

Jake hadn't even had much of a go at driving yet. He knew he'd never be able to show his face back home if he failed remedial.

Most of the other kids were looking a bit nervous too, although there were a few giggling and blowing spit bubbles. They laughed as the bubbles floated around the room before popping on someone's head.

Then the digital screen lit up and again the blown-up head of Gradock covered the wall. Everyone went quiet.

'Good morning, students. Today you will take turns at driving a solo mission. There is an obstacle course set up in the Moon's orbit. The aim is to weave in and out of the moon rocks and come in to land after finishing. No-one is to go past the boundary shield. The far side of the Moon is strictly out of bounds. There will be three cars going at a time. Everyone, please line up.'

Solo? Jake knew he was doomed. The robot made its way down their row. It stopped at each of them and a number lit up on each person's chest. A transparent green number '1' shone on Jake's shirt. Rory's chest was red.

'Number three. Lucky you,' Jake said.

'I'm glad I'm not up first,' Rory answered. He looked at Jake's shirt. The '1' was glowing. 'Oops, sorry.'

'Hey, looks like we're both first,' Skye said to Jake.

She had a green number 1 too. *Maybe going first wouldn't be so bad after all*, Jake thought. Then he looked across the room. Everyone was wearing a red, orange, blue or yellow number, but Jake couldn't see anyone else wearing green. He wondered who the third person would be. Then he noticed Henry making his way to the first car. His chest was glowing green too. Jake almost yelled out 'Moon luck!'

but then remembered that he was supposed to be angry with Henry.

'Beat you over,' Skye said, running to the next car.

Skye was faster than Jake and she chose the third car in the row. Jake took the second car since Henry was already in the front one. Jake engaged the anti-gravity control system and took hold of the throttle. The car started easily and he launched into space behind Henry. Skye followed behind him. Once he had enough lift-off, Jake pulled back the throttle and entered the Moon's orbit. It was almost peaceful up there, with just dark sky and the twinkling of billions of bright stars around him.

He switched on the forward projection screen. Ahead of him, Henry veered around the first moon rock. As Jake came up to it next, he pulled the gear lever to the right and

his space car tilted slightly. He easily cleared the first rock too. He brought up the rear projection screen. Skye was close behind him, and he watched her weave easily around the obstacle.

The next rock came up a bit faster. Henry turned to the left and his car flew past it. Jake was just behind Henry now and he tilted sharply, moving safely past.

Skye was next. Jake held his breath as he watched Skye reach the obstacle through his screen. She seemed pretty close to the rock. The tip of her right wing clipped it but she made it safely through.

The next few rocks were well spaced out and they all glided around them easily. Jake started to relax. But then the course became more difficult. The obstacles were bigger and closer together. The three drivers weaved left, right, right, left and right again, all clearing the rocks. On the last rock Jake felt the bottom of his car scrape the surface. That would have been two points lost in the real space car driving test.

Jake told himself to concentrate harder. He looked around but he couldn't see any more rocks up ahead. Was he getting off-course? Henry had dropped in altitude, so Jake slowed down and dipped the nose of the car downwards, falling in behind him. He could see a snake-like chain of rocks spiralling downwards. Skye was still right behind him. Henry dipped the nose of his car and began swooping over and under them. Jake followed nervously. Vertical obstacles were the hardest. One, two, three. He managed to get around the first few by using the same path as Henry. He wiped his sweaty forehead. Skye also made it through. But just as he was thinking they were on the home stretch, Henry suddenly

50

pulled out and away from the set course.

Jake looked through his forward projection screen, thinking he must be the one going off-course again. But no – it was Henry who had broken away from the course. And he was heading straight towards the boundary shield.

Jake slowed down his space car and tried to think. Why would Henry go out of bounds? Had he become so nervous that he'd messed up the directions? Jake didn't have much time to wonder. He had to decide, quickly, whether to follow Henry or not. He knew he would be in so much trouble for going beyond the shield, but he was also itching to find out what Henry was up to.

Jake took a deep breath and went after Henry.

As he closed in on Henry and the boundary shield, Jake was amazed to see heat spray shoot from the front jets of Henry's space car. Part of the pale yellow shield melted away, leaving a jagged hole. Henry's car passed straight through the gap.

Jake now knew that Henry really did mean to go out of bounds. But why?

He stared at his rear projection screen. Skye was still right behind him. He thought about turning back and saving himself, and Skye, from getting into serious trouble. But this could be his only chance of finding out what was going on. Henry's father's voice came back to him: 'Only one week and you'll be well rewarded. Well rewarded, son.' Could Henry be searching for some kind of treasure on the far side of the Moon?

Jake lined up his car with the gap in the shield, and drove straight through.

He checked his rear screen again and was surprised to see Skye still following him. *Maybe she's as curious as me*, he thought.

Jake saw Henry's car fly in a wide arc. He looked at his OPS screen – the orbit positioning system. They had travelled nearly halfway around the Moon. Henry kept driving. He didn't even seem to notice that Jake and Skye were following. *Maybe he doesn't care*, Jake thought. *Or maybe he wants us to follow him*?

According to the OPS they would reach the far side of the Moon in approximately fifty-eight seconds … twenty-two seconds … one second … and then they were on the far side. Jake began to think this was the worst idea he'd ever had. Not only would he be in trouble with Gradock, again, but Mum and Dad would probably ban him from leaving the space station for the rest of his life.

He looked at his forward projection screen again. There was no sign of Henry, or his space car. Jake started to panic. Where could he be? And how was he ever going to find his way back to the school without Henry to follow? Jake lifted the nose of his car up. All he could see were billions of twinkling stars. Only now it didn't seem so peaceful out here. Instead, the stars just reminded him of how far from anything he really was. He straightened out again, looking to his right and then to his left. There was still no sign of Henry. He looked at the rear projection screen. Skye had the nose of her car pointed almost straight down. Had she found Henry? Then her car disappeared from view.

Jake quickly shifted into a vertical position. Two space cars came into view. He could now see Skye's car and, further away, Henry's. He hit accelerate and chased after them.

As they neared the Moon's surface Jake started to wonder why Henry would break all the rules to come here. The far side was exactly the same as the near side of the Moon. It had the same rocky grey surface. Even the craters seemed the same. Some were small and shallow, others were huge and deep. He was so busy trying to work it all out that he didn't even notice the Moon's surface was coming up fast. Too fast. Not wanting to crash like Henry had the day before, Jake quickly pulled back the controls and righted the car. He sped across the Moon, hovering just above its surface. Skye had levelled out too, and so had Henry. No crash landing for them today.

Jake looked at his forward projection screen again. Henry's car was still travelling just above the Moon's surface. The way he was driving, it seemed as if he knew exactly where he wanted to land, Jake thought. Then something huge and dark came into view. Jake pulled to the right. It looked like a massive crater. No, it couldn't be! Jake had never seen a hole so huge. And the edges weren't like those of a normal crater. There were great big chunks cut out of the gaping hole.

Jake pushed the altitude lever up a bit, not wanting to be sucked into the hole. Coming up closer, he could see he was right. It wasn't a normal crater at all. It looked like the inside of a massive ice-cream cone planted in the ground. What could it be? He pushed on the accelerate button but nothing happened. The button had jammed. He tried again. Still nothing. Then suddenly he was thrown forward and the space car came to a complete stop. Jake hit the start key but the motor had stopped.

Oh no, this can't be happening, he thought.

He'd broken down somewhere on the far side of the Moon. What was he going to do? Then he remembered Skye. She was sure to notice what had happened and would help. Jake looked in the projection screen but she had also come to a complete stop. Further ahead he saw that Henry's car was also still. Just as he was starting to think they'd all be lost forever, with no way of getting back, his communication screen lit up.

Gradock's face came into view. Phew! Jake was glad the remedial school knew his space car was in trouble. But Gradock's row of crystal teeth wasn't shining in a smile. Instead, he scowled angrily, which made him look more like a mushroom than ever.

'All space car systems have been shut down. The three of you have flown out of bounds. You will be taken back to the driving school immediately.'

The screen went blank once more. Jake started to feel a churning in his stomach. He reached for a space sickness bag and spewed up the entire contents of that morning's gooey breakfast cereal. He was in *so* much trouble. He wondered what Skye was thinking. Jake could see three of the school's space cars heading straight for them. One flew under each of the space cars. He felt a sudden jerk. The control panel lit up and the manual override took over. 'Magnetic field now engaged,' a computerised voice said. Jake felt his space car begin to turn around. He was being towed back to the school.

Skye, Henry and Jake stood in Gradock's office. Jake had never been in this much trouble in all his years at school. The only time he'd been sent to the principal's office was when he accidentally let off an exploding space goop bomb in class last year, ruining his teacher's reports. But this time it was much worse.

Jake waited for Gradock to appear on the digital imaging screen to tell them they were

all expelled from remedial school. Skye looked just as nervous as Jake felt. She kept hopping from foot to foot. Henry seemed worried too. Even though it was hard to tell with him, the fact that he was counting to one hundred over and over under his breath was probably a pretty good sign he was scared out of his brain.

After what felt like ten light years, Gradock's face finally appeared on his office screen.

'Sit down,' he said gruffly.

Skye, Henry and Jake slumped into the orange plastic chairs behind them.

'As you all know, the far side of the Moon is strictly out of bounds to all students. I made this very clear, didn't I?'

'Yes, sir, I'm sorry ...' Skye started to say.

But Gradock wasn't listening to excuses and he kept talking. 'I will speak to each of you in person and make my decision about what to do with the three of you after that.'

Skye and Jake looked at each other. Jake knew they were both wondering what the other would say. Jake felt really bad about getting her into trouble.

Henry saw Gradock first, then Skye went in next. After an awful wait, Jake was finally called into the office. He was surprised at how much smaller Gradock looked in real life.

'Why don't you tell me what happened, Jake?'

Gradock stared at him and Jake wondered again what Skye had said. Most of all, he couldn't imagine how Henry had tried to explain why he had burned a hole through the boundary shield and driven across to the far side of the Moon.

'Well, sir, I was following Henry's course and just somehow ended up on the far side,' Jake explained quietly.

'You mean to tell me you *accidentally* drove through the hole Henry made in the boundary shield?' Gradock asked.

'Um … yes?' Jake said, knowing his excuse sounded exactly like what it was – a great big lie.

'I find that very hard to believe. It would have been quite difficult to drive through such a small gap. So, how about you tell me the truth now and we might be able to sort all this out?'

Gradock leaned forward to listen. Jake wanted to tell him the whole story. About Henry's dad telling him he'd be well rewarded. About how he had followed Henry that night, and about finding that strange crater. But part of him was worried that it would just get him into more trouble.

'Well, sir, the truth is I was just curious. I've been wondering what the far side looks like because no-one ever goes there. So when the chance came up I just followed Henry.'

Gradock looked surprised. 'Then the three of you didn't decide to go to the far side together? Before taking off?'

'No, sir,' Jake said, truthfully. 'I just followed Henry and Skye just followed me.'

'Hmmm. It's hard to know what to believe.' He scratched the scar on his chin as though he was trying to decide what to do with Jake.

Then Gradock smiled and said, in a low voice, 'And what *did* you think of the far side, Jake? Once you were there, did you see anything *different*? *Unusual* perhaps?'

'Ah, no sir. It looked exactly the same as the near side. Maybe a bit rockier,' Jake said quickly, picturing that huge cone-shaped hole in the ground. He hoped Gradock couldn't see through his lie.

Gradock seemed to relax a bit and his

64

crystal teeth shone through his gums in a half smile.

'Well, the crust on the far side is a little thicker. That's all. Usually I would expel any student who broke such an important rule. You could have gotten lost, or crashed, or even have been killed. It's my job to teach students to drive in space and it's also my job to keep them safe. But I do understand curiosity, Jake. I was a curious child myself. Always roaming off. I guess that's why I was a triple-ace pilot on Earth. That's until some people decided they didn't like the way I drove ...' Gradock's face turned dark.

Jake wondered why Gradock was teaching at a remedial driving school on the Moon if he had been a triple-ace pilot on Earth. But Gradock stopped talking, as though he'd just realised Jake was there, and smiled again.

'Never mind me. I'm willing to give you a

second chance, young Jake. But one more mistake and you're out, okay?'

'Okay,' Jake gulped, knowing how lucky he'd been.

66

The next two days passed by without much happening. Jake concentrated on getting his practice scores up, and he got better and better at driving without hitting anything. Henry gave him some useful tips in group practice and Jake started to feel confident that he could pass the test. The only thing left to work on was precision flying. Jake found it hard to keep in line with other cars. Still, everyone started to relax as their driving improved and they even took turns racing each other around the course on the last day before the test. Jake had almost forgotten about Henry. He was spending lots of time studying quietly and hadn't snuck out onto the Moon again. If anything, he seemed to study harder than anyone else. Jake began to think he had been silly for thinking there was anything odd going on with Henry.

Finally, testing day arrived.

The theory test was first. Jake sat nervously at his desk. He couldn't seem to read the control panel diagrams and angles for landing. Every time he entered an answer in his notebook with his laser pen, it flashed red. The way things were going he knew he'd be lucky to even pass the theory test, let alone get a chance to drive in the practical. *If Henry thinks he gets nervous flying, he should see me on testing day*, Jake thought. Back home, no matter how much he'd studied, he still got so nervous he failed his tests. It looked like today wasn't going to be any different.

He tried to focus on the questions on the screen but the answers still wouldn't come. Then he remembered something that Henry had said – that he didn't get nervous when he was in the simulator because he knew it was fake. So Jake pretended his test was a simulated one too. *It's just a practice test,* he said to himself. It was then that the answers started coming to him more easily and his notebook started to flash green. Jake finished the test with a score of 26 out of 30, and two minutes to spare.

After the test, Jake sat with his friends in the lunchroom, talking about how they all went. They all wore the medals Gradock had given them for passing the theory test. Milly and Skye scored 30 out of 30, and even Rory scored 28.

'You girls must have cheated off each other to get all the answers right,' Rory complained.

'No, we just studied hard,' Milly argued.

'Humph!' he replied.

Even though Jake had scored the lowest of them all, it had still been a proud moment when Gradock pinned his medal to his shirt. Gradock had given Jake a smile and even winked at him as he shook his hand. Jake forgot all about how angry Gradock had been when Jake got in trouble for going out of bounds.

Now it was just the practical driving after lunch. That was the part they were now most nervous about.

'Hey, where's Henry?' Skye suddenly exclaimed.

They looked around the room. There was no sign of him. In all their excitement about passing their test, they hadn't even noticed that he wasn't in the lunchroom with them. Jake realised he hadn't been there when they were given their medals, either. Jake looked over at Rory.

'I bet I know where he's gone,' Jake said.

Rory and Jake both got up, leaving Milly and Skye to finish their lunch.

Jake went straight to the hidden exit he had seen Henry use on their first night at remedial school, but there was no sign of him.

'I was sure he'd have come here,' Jake said.

'Where else could he be?' Rory asked.

Jake wasn't sure. Then he had an idea. 'I know!' he said.

They raced back down the corridor. They reached the space car loading zone and looked around. There was still no sign of Henry.

'I thought he might have taken one of the cars out,' Jake sighed.

'Come on! Let's get back. The prac will be starting soon,' Rory pleaded.

'No, he's *got* to be somewhere,' Jake insisted.

'Well, I'm going back.'

But just as Rory turned to go he saw something move beside one of the space cars. Jake grabbed Rory by the arm.

'That's him. He's heading for one of the space cars,' he whispered.

'Where?' Rory asked.

'Shhh!'

Jake crouched down and motioned for Rory to follow. They sneaked along behind the loading zone pylons. Henry stopped in front of one of the space cars. He took something out of his pocket and pointed it at the car. The entry hatch opened.

'Quick! Let's go!'

'But how did he open ...' Rory started to say.

Before Jake could answer, they heard footsteps.

'Hey!' someone hissed.

Oh no, Jake thought, *we've been caught!* Now they'd never be able to find out what Henry was really up to. He slowly turned around.

'You're not going anywhere without us.'

Jake smiled. It was Milly and Skye.

'Hurry up then,' he whispered.

Skye threw Rory and Jake a space suit each.

'You might need these,' she smiled.

Grateful for her quick thinking, the boys pulled on their suits. The girls were already dressed in theirs. Meanwhile, Henry had slid underneath the space car. He seemed to be doing a safety check on it.

'Now's our chance,' Jake said quietly.

The four ran up to the car and sneaked in through the entry hatch. They quickly hid behind the back passenger seats. A minute later Henry took his place in the driver's seat and started up the car.

They lifted off and Henry started flying.

They had no idea where Henry was going, and it quickly started to feel cramped with all four of them crouched down at the back. The leg Jake was sitting on started to go numb. Luckily, Henry's expert driving made it easy for them to keep their places without toppling into each other, or floating up and being seen. Jake wondered again how Henry had ended up at remedial school.

Soon Jake felt the car start to lean in to the left. He realised they must be coming in to land. He was pushed against Rory as they tilted further and could feel Skye's arm pressed against his. Soon they were all squashed into the side of the space car. Jake started to get nervous. What would Henry do when they landed? What if he found out they'd followed him? But more than anything he wondered what Henry was doing and where he was going. Jake pictured the huge cone in the ground again. He was becoming even more sure than ever that it wasn't an ordinary crater. *I bet that's where we're going now,* he thought.

The car came to a stop. Jake heard the hatch open and a gush of air came in. Then he heard the thump of footsteps on metal. They got quieter and then couldn't be heard at all. Skye was the first to decide it was safe to come out from their hiding spots. She climbed over the back seat.

'All clear,' she whispered.

Rory and Milly climbed over to the front as well. Jake stood up but his leg had gone

all wobbly from sitting on it. He gave it a rub and the feeling came back. When he finally managed to climb over, he found everyone else staring out of the front window of the car with their mouths open, like three goldfish stuck in a fishbowl. They were looking at Henry, who was walking across the Moon's surface.

Jake almost laughed, knowing they were seeing what he had that first night. 'Let me guess. No space suit?'

'That's impossible!' Rory exclaimed.

'If he were *human*,' Skye said. 'I thought it all along, but now I'm sure. Henry's a cyborg.'

'A *what*?' Milly said, looking terrified.

'He's part-human, part-robot. He has to be.'

'There's no such thing. You've been reading too many stories,' Rory argued.

'How else could he survive out on the Moon with no breathing gear?' she snapped back.

'She's right,' Jake said. 'Robots are used for

mining and space exploration all the time.'

'It would explain why he talks so weird,' Milly said.

'And why he can drive so well. I bet he's not really a student at all,' Jake added.

'Remember when you gave him a slap on the back, Rory? You said yourself he felt like metal,' Skye said.

'I didn't mean he was *really* made of metal.' But Rory didn't look so sure anymore.

'Whatever he is, we'd better get going now or we'll lose him,' Jake said, catching sight of Henry bouncing across the rocky ground.

The four friends started to follow Henry. But they found that sneaking after him wasn't so easy to do when there were four of them and they were all wearing big bulky space suits. They bounced their way across the dusty ground. It was just lucky Henry was so focused on where he was going or he would have noticed them for sure. Then he stopped. The four of them crouched down behind a big pile of moon rocks and watched as Henry walked right up to the edge of a crater. It was the same ice-cream cone hole in the ground that Jake had seen last time he was here. He looked back at the space car. It was just a shimmering speck in the distance. When he turned back again Henry had disappeared.

'Where's he gone?'

'Into the crater,' Milly cried, amazed.

They came out from their hiding spot and went closer to the massive black pit. Jake gasped. It was so big that if the cone was filled with ice-cream it would take the whole year to eat it all. And there was nothing natural about it. The walls of the pit were made of metal.

'What *is* this thing?' Rory asked.

No-one had an answer.

'Hey! Over here,' Skye called out.

Jake was the first to reach her. He found her lying on her stomach with her arms dangling over the side of the crater.

'Be careful!' he yelled.

'Swing my legs over, Jake,' Skye replied.

'Have you gone space mad? It's too dangerous.'

'Quickly!' she insisted.

Jake leaned over with the idea of pulling her out and saving her from sliding into the crater. But as he peered in he saw what she had found.

'That's where he went,' Skye said, pointing to a long metal ladder that was attached to the wall of the crater. 'Come on, we've got to follow him.'

Jake helped her and Skye started climbing down the ladder. He had no idea what they were getting themselves into. As he started climbing down he heard Milly and Rory arguing.

'I can't!' Rory cried.

'Yes, you can,' Milly insisted.

'No, I can't.'

'Just don't look down.'

Jake knew they couldn't lose Henry now so he left them to sort it out. Then he heard the clunk of more boots on the metal rungs. Milly must have got Rory to climb down after all.

Finally, Jake reached the bottom of the ladder. He stepped onto a metal platform next to Skye. They were right inside the crater, or whatever it was. The hole had become narrower as they climbed down and now he could feel a chill even through his space suit. Rory and Milly reached the bottom of the crater next.

'That wasn't so bad, hey?' Rory said, his voice sounding shaky.

'I told you,' Milly replied.

'Shhh!' Skye commanded.

'Where to now?' Jake whispered.

'Through here,' Skye replied.

There was an opening in the wall. It was dark but it was the only place that Henry could have gone. Jake followed Skye, with Rory and Milly close behind.

They all felt their way along in the dark. It was like walking through a cave. The walls were solid and the tunnel was so narrow Jake felt his shoulders brush against its sides. It was hard to keep quiet as their boots thudded on the metal floor.

Eventually Jake saw light up ahead. Part of him wanted to turn back and run to the safety of the space car, but he knew they had to find out what the crater was, and what Henry was up to. Jake began to think he should have told Gradock everything he knew about Henry after all. But somewhere inside he still believed he had been right not to.

Suddenly Skye stuck her arm out to stop Jake, and they all banged into each other like bowling pins.

'Ouch! That's my foot,' Milly cried.

'Sorry,' Rory said.

'*Shhh*!' Skye repeated.

They all shuffled in closer to see. Jake gasped and Skye clapped her hand over his mouth. They'd reached the end of the tunnel. In front of them was something that looked like a huge underground space station. All around the walls there were panels and dials and screens. None of it made any sense to Jake. Then he saw that Henry was there too, standing with his back to them. In front of him a screen displayed a gigantic image of the Moon and the Earth. The four friends stayed hidden in the darkness of the tunnel. Meanwhile, Henry pressed several buttons. Suddenly he stopped.

Without turning around he said, 'I wondered how long it would take you to get here.'

None of them moved. How long had Henry known they'd been following him?

'You might as well come out of there,' Henry said.

They all looked at one another. Rory pushed Jake in the back and he stumbled forward.

'I'm not going up to him,' Jake whispered.

'You're the one who brought us here,' Rory argued.

'So?'

Skye sighed. 'You boys are such wimps.' She boldly walked right up to Henry. Jake wished he was that gutsy.

'What is this place?' Skye asked Henry.

'Yeah, and who are you?' Jake added, trying to sound braver than he felt.

'And *what* are you?' Rory demanded, suddenly acting a lot tougher.

Only Milly kept quiet.

'What are you doing here?' Skye added.

'You are all very inquisitive,' Henry stated.

Jake didn't tell him he had about five million more questions he'd like to ask. Then, to everyone's horror, Henry turned over his wrist and started pulling at the skin on his arm.

'Stop!' Jake yelled.

But as Henry pulled back the skin, he revealed something that looked like a mini-control system underneath.

'He *is* a cyborg!' Rory exclaimed.

Skye raised her eyebrows at Rory as if to say 'I told you so.'

'Yes. I am. I'm still a bit human but many parts of me are mechanical now.'

'How is that possible?' Rory cried.

'I'm from the CIA,' he said.

'The *what*?' Jake said.

'The CIA hasn't existed for hundreds of years,' Skye protested.

'Except in the movies,' Rory mumbled.

'CIA stands for Central Intergalactic Agency. I had a space car accident. The CIA doctors saved me by giving me some robotic parts.'

'Wow!' Jake exclaimed. 'But what does that have to do with remedial school?'

'I've been on a mission to track Gradock for six years, two days, five hours and eleven seconds. Twelve seconds. Thir– but I don't have much time. Let me show you.'

Henry pulled open a tiny chamber on the panel in his arm and pulled out a long lead. He held the end between his fingers and plugged it into a socket in front of the screen. Skye, Rory and Jake stood frozen to the spot as he started punching in more numbers. He was moving faster than the speed of light, or that's how it looked as his fingers blurred across the screen. Now Jake understood why Henry was so hopeless at acting like he couldn't drive. Jake realised that with those skills he must be one of the best drivers in the universe.

'Not so fast!' Milly yelled.

She surprised everyone by running forward, pushing Jake and the others aside and leaping onto Henry's back. She started hitting him with her fists. He twisted from side to side, trying to get her off but she held on tight with her legs. Finally he reached behind him and pulled her off.

'Hey!' Skye cried.

'How do we know he's who he says he is?' Milly asked.

Jake realised she was right. They had no idea what he was doing there, or what he was up to. Why was he messing around with the computers? They all tried to wrestle Henry away from the screen. He tried to push them away and as he did he stretched out his arm. He pressed a big green button in the centre of the console.

For a moment they were all stunned. Jake thought quickly. Whatever Henry had set off, he knew it had to be stopped. There was a red button right next to the green one. While Rory and Skye were trying to pull Henry away from the console, Jake pressed it.

'*Noooooooo!*' Henry screamed, trying to

wriggle free from Rory and Skye. 'Don't you know what you've just done? The sequence will take another ten minutes to reprogram. Gradock's sure to get here before then.'

'Let's hope so,' Rory sighed.

'*Please.* Listen. You see this?' he asked, pointing at the picture of the Moon and Earth on the screen.

'Yes,' they said.

'This is Gradock's launch sequence.'

'It can't be …' Skye gasped.

She seemed to have understood something none of the rest of them had. Jake looked up at the screen. It showed the simulated path of the Moon. Then Jake knew what was happening.

'The Moon's heading straight towards Earth!' he exclaimed. 'But how?'

'We're inside a giant booster,' Skye cried.

'That's what this ice-cream cone hole is? A

massive rocket?' Jake said, shocked.

'Exactly. And now that you've stopped me the launch sequence will continue as Gradock planned. An explosion will take place in approximately six minutes, shifting the Moon out of orbit and sending it straight for the Earth.'

'But Gradock … '

'It was my mission to stop him from carrying out his plan. The launch sequence had already started when I got here. I was trying to reprogram the launch to shift the Moon's orbit further, so it would miss the Earth.'

'But we'd still all be destroyed,' Rory said. 'Great plan!'

'Yes, but it could only be stopped completely using the control unit that triggered it. Gradock is the only one who has it. This way, at least the Earth would still be saved.'

'And now?'

A voice came from behind them: 'Now the Moon will hit the Earth's surface, destroying all life on the planet.'

They all turned and gasped at once: 'Gradock!'

'Thank you for explaining it all, Henry. And now, if you'll excuse me, your services are no longer required,' Gradock said coolly.

Then he grabbed Henry by the arm. Henry tried to pull away but Gradock was too quick. He reached into the panel on Henry's arm and pulled out a plug. Henry was suddenly frozen with one arm raised above his head. He'd been shut down.

'*No!*' Jake screamed.

'I'd love to stay and chat but I'm in a bit of a hurry. I'm glad you followed Henry for me, though. If you hadn't followed him I would never have known he was on to me already.'

'What do you mean?' Jake said.

'The medals I gave everyone for passing the theory test. Yours have been implanted with tracking devices. Luckily, once the devices alerted me to where Henry was heading, I was able to start the launch sequence from my office.'

The kids looked at the medals they'd been wearing proudly on their shirts. They hadn't been given as rewards at all.

'But why would you want to destroy the Earth?' Jake asked.

'And the Moon?' Skye added.

'They all deserve to be wiped out. I should be exploring the entire universe, driving from

 94

planet to planet. Instead, I'm stuck here, on the Moon, teaching you kids space car driving.'

Jake remembered Gradock in his office that day, talking about how he was a triple-ace pilot on Earth, and something about him getting in trouble for his flying. If only Jake had known then how angry he was about it …

'They think I'm "too reckless" to be a space explorer. Pah! Just because I hit a few space stations.' Gradock's face turned purple.

Then he calmed down and turned to read the control panel screen. 'Three minutes left. Now, if you'll excuse me, I think I'll go somewhere warm for my little vacation. I deserve it after putting up with children for twenty-one years.'

With the deadly control unit counting down the seconds in his hands, he backed away and slipped into the dark tunnel.

'You can try and chase me but I don't think

a bunch of remedial kids have much chance against a triple-ace pilot. Do you?' His laugh echoed back towards them as he disappeared into the tunnel.

'What do we do now?' Rory cried.

'Should we try and get Henry going again?' Milly suggested.

'It would take too long to try and figure out. And even if we could, we'd still have to work out how to stop Gradock,' Skye said.

Jake suddenly realised exactly what was happening. His parents. His friends. They were all about to be destroyed in a giant explosion. The only answer was to save them all. But how? Jake closed his eyes and sent a telepathic message to his mum. She picked up on everything. She *had* to get the message in time.

'This is no time to space out,' Rory said, giving Jake a shove. 'Let's go!'

  96

With a quick glance back at the still figure of Henry, Jake ran back along the tunnel with the others following close behind. They jumped into the space car Henry had taken and Jake started the engine.

'Can you see where Gradock went?' Jake asked.

'He's gone already,' Milly cried.

'We've got to figure out which way he flew,' Rory said.

'I bet he's headed for my home,' Skye said.

'Venus?' Rory asked, frowning.

'Didn't he say he wanted to have his holiday somewhere warm?'

'Yes, but ...'

'Venus is our best shot,' Jake said, pulling the space car to the left and accelerating as much as he could.

Jake stared out through the front projection screen but all he could see were stars and a few asteroids floating around. Milly and Skye were huddled around the front projection screen too while Rory kept a lookout at the back.

'Anything?' Jake asked, knowing the answer wasn't going to be good.

'Nothing,' Milly and Skye replied.

'Not behind us either,' Rory added. 'How long have we got?'

'Two minutes and ten seconds,' Skye said.

They sped along in silence, thinking they were going to be too late.

'Wait!' Skye suddenly cried. 'To your right!'

Jake made a sharp turn and Gradock's space car came into view.

'We found him!' Milly cried.

'Now what?' Rory said.

'We'll have to get close enough to engage a magnetic field. Do you think you can do it, Jake?'

'I can try,' Jake said, unsure.

He concentrated harder than he'd ever done before and drove in as close as he could to Gradock's space car until they were nose to tail.

'Okay, I'm going to try and drive under him,' Jake told the others. 'Then I can flip us over and use the emergency escape hatch to get into Gradock's car. I need you to tell me when I'm right underneath, Rory.'

'You got it.'

Getting that close to Gradock without bumping his car was hard, but Jake knew trying to flip the space car so the hatches lined up was going to be even tougher.

As if reading his thoughts, Skye said, 'You

can do it, Jake. I know you can.'

He took a deep breath. 'Here we go. Everyone strapped in?'

'Go!' they all replied.

Jake pulled the lever all the way to the right. The car tilted sideways. Jake held the lever steady and the space car flipped over. They all hung like bats from the top of the space car.

'Seatbelt release,' Milly said, pushing a button.

Their belts retracted and they floated upwards. They somersaulted over. Everything looked weird upside down.

'How long?' Rory asked, anxiously.

'One minute and forty seconds,' Skye said. 'I'll engage the magnetic field once we're close enough to Gradock.'

'Okay!' he said, still not quite believing he had just managed to pull off his first ever upside-down manoeuvre.

The control panel was now above the front screen. Jake reached up and shifted the control lever forward gently, trying to get the space car close enough to Gradock's. His palms felt slippery on the controls and his vision blurred as he tried to line the two cars up. Then Rory stepped in to help.

'Bit higher,' Rory said, looking through the viewer screen.

Jake pushed the control lever further forward.

'Almost there,' he said.

Jake pushed a little harder on the lever.

'That's got it!' Rory said, smiling. 'Now go forward a bit. The escape hatches are almost lined up.'

Jake pushed the lever gently.

'A tiny bit more. And … stop!'

Skye busied herself at the central control panel. 'Okay! Let's hope this is right.' She pressed a bright blue button and the car's computerised voice said, 'Magnetic field now engaged.'

The space car jerked upwards.

'I'd say that worked,' Rory said, smiling for the first time since they had climbed down that metal ladder.

Their excitement didn't last long as they all realised they now had to actually get the control unit off Gradock and stop the Moon rocketing into the Earth in less than a minute's time.

Rory pulled open the escape hatch. 'You first,' he said to Jake.

'Just because I drove,' Jake mumbled as he allowed himself to float towards the hatch's opening.

The hatch under Gradock's car opened easily and Jake quietly pulled himself up through the narrow opening into his space car. Gradock spun around as soon as Jake got to his feet.

'Thirty seconds to go,' Gradock said, reading the master control unit. 'Not a bad effort!'

'Yeah, you were right about one thing. Teamwork *is* important.'

'Are you sure you don't want to join me on my little holiday?'

'Not a chance!' Jake said.

'And now, if you'll excuse *us*,' Rory piped up.

Everyone had now made it through the hatch and Rory seemed to have found his nerve. 'It's four against one. Hand over the control unit.'

Gradock smirked like he knew they had no chance of stopping him in time. His crystal teeth glowed menacingly. 'Ha, try it! I dare you.'

Rory gestured to Milly: '*Now!*'

Milly threw a green egg-shaped object. It hit Gradock on the head and cracked open. Slooper Goo oozed out of it and he was soon covered from head to foot in green goo. He tried to wriggle free but the goo held him tight. Jake was impressed. That was even stickier than the stuff his mum had used at home when he got his remedial letter. His mouth hung open in amazement.

'It's the new Slooper Goo 2,' she said.

Jake closed his mouth again.

'Is about twenty seconds long enough to hold him?'

'You bet!' Milly said.

Skye raced forward and pulled the unit from Gradock's gooey hand.

'Which one?' she asked, staring at the unit with a trembling hand.

Jake leaped over. The counter was down to ten seconds. There were so many buttons he wasn't sure which one to press.

'Try that huge black one in the middle,' Jake finally guessed.

Skye nodded and pressed the button. Nothing happened. There were just four seconds to go. Three. Two. One. It was all over. The Moon would start heading towards Earth at any moment. Then suddenly the screen went black.

'Ahhhhhhhh!' Skye screamed. She wrapped her arms around Jake's neck. 'We did it!'

'What?' he asked. But then he realised. They'd done it. The launch sequence had stopped.

They all started jumping around and screaming like a bunch of space bugs. Then Jake heard a clanging noise from below.

'What's that?' Milly asked, worried.

Three heads suddenly appeared at the hatch.

'Is everyone okay in here?' It was Henry, and Henry's parents, who Jake now knew probably weren't really his parents at all.

'Will and Bree,' Henry said, gesturing to

the man and woman as though that explained it all.

'The booster launch has somehow been stopped,' Will said.

'Mission successfully completed,' Henry added, grinning.

'Just one small problem,' Jake said.

'What?' Henry and his pretend parents said together.

Jake looked over at the stunned figure of Gradock. His muscles were starting to twitch as the goop began to melt.

'Don't worry about him,' Bree said. She pulled a gold lasso from her belt and threw it across the room towards Gradock. It opened up into a kind of parachute and covered him completely. Jake wondered how such fine thread could possibly hold him.

'It's space spider web,' Skye said in awe.

Gradock's eyes flickered open.

'You're under arrest by the CIA,' Will said. Then he turned to the four friends. 'Well done, everyone. We never thought we'd get here in time. If it weren't for you the Earth would have been destroyed by now.'

'And the Moon,' Skye added.

'Yes, and the Moon.'

'But how did you know where we were?' Jake began.

'Thanks to that telepathic message you sent to your mum we were able to find your exact location. With a little help from Henry we read your thought pattern and found you.'

'How did you fix him?' Skye asked.

'Yeah, he was completely shut down when we left,' Rory added.

'A quick reboot did the trick,' Bree said, winking.

'What about Henry? What happens now the mission is completed?'

'I'll go back to CIA headquarters for my next assignment,' Henry answered.

'It'll be sad to see him go,' Will said, turning to Henry. 'You've been just like a real son to me.'

'Thanks … Dad.'

Will seemed lost in thought until Bree interrupted, 'Ah, I think you've got something to say.'

'Oh yes. Milly, Skye, Rory and Jake, I give you your space car licences. For a bunch of remedial kids, that was some pretty impressive driving. I've never seen a kid your age pull off an inverted move like yours, Jake. And the teamwork, amazing. Our CIA pilots could learn a thing or two about working so well as a unit.'

They all laughed. Right at that moment, Jake would be happy if he never drove again.

Jake was quiet on the trip home. His head was full of all that had happened over the past week. Plus, it was a bit weird just being a passenger again after the excitement of flying through space. Mum and Dad were doing enough talking for him anyway. They were busy arguing about where he got his excellent flying genes from.

'No, no no. His flying skills are clearly from me,' Mum said. 'How else do you think I got

110

him to school on time all these years?'

'Ah, but he's just like his dad. Failing several times before mastering space car driving.'

'I didn't fail fifty four times,' Jake interrupted.

'See? It's not the same as you at all. He gets his driving skills from me,' Mum said, turning to smile at Jake.

'Look out!' Jake screamed.

Mum quickly pulled back, just missing the car in front.

'Oops!'

No-one said any more after that until Mum slid into their hangar, scraping the side wall slightly before coming to a stop. It made Jake even happier that he would be able to drive himself to school from now on. He quickly exited the car and went inside. When he looked on the kitchen table he saw there was a letter waiting for him. His name blazed in red, fiery letters on the envelope. When he picked up the letter the tiny flames disappeared, leaving black, jagged writing. He hastily pulled out the letter and read it.

'Well, what does it say?' Dad asked.

'It's ... it's ...' Jake could hardly get the words out.

Mum snatched it from his hand and scanned the letter. 'It's a letter from the Rocket Battles race organisers. Jake's been invited as a wildcard entry for next year's race. He'd be making up a team with his remedial friends.'

Jake hopped up and down excitedly. This was better than great. The Rocket Battles were the ultimate in race car driving. Only the best racers from the solar system were invited to take part. There was always an extra wildcard team invited as well. He couldn't believe he and his friends had been chosen. This was really turning out to be the best day ever.

'Wow, I can't wait,' Jake cried.

'That's a dangerous race,' Dad said, frowning.

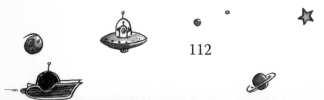

'You're much too young,' Mum added.

'But Mum, Dad, I know I can do it. We can – Milly, Rory, Skye and me,' Jake insisted.

'I'm sorry Jake, but there's no way we can allow you to go in it. You could get hurt,' Mum added.

She scrunched the letter up into a ball but the letter stuck fast to her hand.

'What's this?' she exclaimed.

'Slooper Goo 2,' Jake smiled. 'I thought you might react this way.'

Jake's parents tried hard not to grin back but he saw the edges of their lips curling into a smile.

'Okay, we'll see, Jake,' Mum replied, 'Now please get me some neon gas to get this stuff off my hand.'

Jake ran into the kitchen, knowing his next adventure was about to begin.

ABOUT THE AUTHOR

Candice's quirky style, fast-paced narratives and originality appeals to reluctant boy readers in particular.

Following several years working in the media, Candice now devotes her time to her writing and to raising her two young daughters. She is also a Literacy Champion for the Municipal Literacy Partnership Program (MLPP).